If Dogs Had Wings

To Faye and Ben Gibbons—dog people, of course; and to
Chris Demarest for giving wings to a dream
                    —L. D. B.

To all the Buddies of the world
                    —C. L. D.

Published by Caroline House
Boyds Mills Press, Inc.
A Highlights Company
815 Church Street
Honesdale, Pennsylvania 18431
Printed in Mexico

Publisher Cataloging-in-Publication Data
Brimner, Larry Dane.
    If dogs had wings / by Larry Dane Brimner ; illustrated by Chris L. Demarest.—1st ed.
[32]p. : col. ill. ; cm.
Summary : A dog imagines what the world would be like if dogs had wings.
ISBN 1-56397-146-1
1. Dogs—Fiction—Juvenile literature. [1. Dogs—Fiction.]
I. Demarest, Chris L., ill. II. Title.
    [E]-dc20   1996   AC   CIP
Library of Congress Catalog Card Number 95-80776

First edition, 1996
Book designed by Tim Gillner
The text of this book is set in 16-point Stone Serif.
The illustrations are done in watercolors.

10 9 8 7 6 5 4 3 2 1

Larry Dane Brimner

IF DOGS HAD WINGS

Illustrated by Chris L. Demarest

Boyds Mills Press

When a dog looks out,
the world is long and low . . .

and way up high.

A room is a forest of legs. . . .

Stairs are a mighty mountain. . . .

And a street stretches out
in an endless black ribbon.

But if dogs had wings,
the world would not be so big.

Legs would become people,
squat and stubby. . . .

Stairs would become lookouts,
high and lofty. . . .

And a street would be a braid
decorating the land.

If dogs had wings,
they would fly out the window
to soar with planes.

They would perform loop-the-loops
and spins
and rolls.

They would glide above meadows, flushing out pheasants.

And they would perch in trees
to welcome the dawn.

The calico around the corner wouldn't be so bold.

Neither would puddles dampen their feet.

If dogs had wings,
they'd fly to the moon
to howl at the earth
and chase falling stars.

They would find their special families
so far below,
and see their bowls,
mere specks,
waiting outside the door.

Then weary and hungry
(and feeling lonely),
they'd sail through space
to be welcomed home
by a friendly hug,
a pat on the head,
and a goody to gobble.

A quilt,
soft and snugly,
would beckon them to the corner
for a yawn . . .

and a stretch . . .

and a much-needed snooze—
if dogs had wings.

If only dogs had wings.